THE
SHELL LADY

She collected shells but discovered lost voices

MIKE PEARCE

ISBN:10-1530923778
ISBN-13:978-1530923779

DEDICATION

This book is dedicated to all those who feel that
certain objects when held or touched can induce
certain satisfaction and even a close kind of unity
within the human psyche.

CONTENTS

Acknowledgments

ACKNOWLEDGMENTS

The author would like to thank Christine Pearce for checking the manuscript. He would also like to thank Joan Bull, manager of the British Red Cross charity shop in Deal, Kent, for sale of the shell mosaic which is shown on the front cover.

.

1 INTRODUCTION

We've often seen small, wonderful items in seaside shops made out of shells. They can be figures of animals and even boats. Annie was an expert at making these out of the shells which she collected every day from the beach. Her speciality was in making shell women, their dresses made out of scallops and the bonnet out of large cockles.

One day she found something floating in the tide which would change her life completely and even help generate a famous landmark in her little seaside town. Many of us, holding an object, can relate this to our own memories or visualise the owner's possible appreciation of this object. This story goes beyond this, releasing the very energy stored in everyday objects with voices from the past.

2 ANNIE AND THE SHELLS

Annie was the youngest of twelve children. She was
not very tall but was the only one to have flowing
ginger locks of hair. She never did very well at school
but was always collecting things where she lived near
the seaside. In her free time she would collect pieces
of wood and, most of all, shells from the beach. She
lived near the chalk cliff. She wanted so much to find
a piece of ambergris from a whale's intestine on her
beach but every item she picked up was always an
orange stone.

She was always dressed in black, with a white bonnet
with white frills and black ties. Her black cotton dress
was longer at the back so would drag in the wet sand
whilst she looked for shells. This left white salt marks
all over it. She always took with her, when she went
to the beach, a red bag and a small metal rake. This
was the kind you would get for children as part of a
set with a small spade and brightly painted bucket.
She had found the rake at the edge of a rock pool just
near the harbour. Every day when the tides were right
she would collect shells on the beach. Different parts
of the beach had different mixtures of sand, stones
and shells. One area had very fine sand where lots of
small cowries would wash up into the fine channels
made when the tide ran back to the sea. In this place

there also were many fine different coloured flattened tellins. Around the harbour near the slip way she would find razor shellfish. As a child with her brother, as the tide receded she used to see bubbles emerging from small holes in the sand. By pouring salt on top of these burrows they would force the razor fish, who thought the salty sea water had returned, up to the surface and they dug them out quickly. The insides were used by herself and her brother as bait for fishing and any extra would be bundled up to bring home for her uncle to cook and eat. She would use the empty shells for her models. In storms often hundreds of these empty razor shells were washed onto the shore into pools, which she gathered up.

Under the life boat slip with its rusting metal girders plunging down into the sand right out into the sea, were huge bunches of mussels. These were of all sizes and attached by their strong fibres to the metal. Many empty shells lay scattered on the sand below. Around the base of the lifeboat slip were also colonies of sabella worms forming forests of hard tubes just above the sand level. If broken, the red worms would be exposed but soon retreated into their tubes. Near the island which was based just off the shore and surrounded by many rocks she would be able to find empty limpet shells as well as winkles and whelks which were often dislodged by rough tides.

Under this part of the shore was underlying chalk. There were high chalk cliffs behind her, their layers visible and studded with lines of flint. Each inch of chalk was said to represent two thousand five hundred years and by climbing up the steps to the promenade one was passing through a vast period of geological history. On the beach most areas of chalk had many winkles all over them like currants in sponge cake when seen from a distance. The sides of the chalk were washed clean exposing fresh chalk at each tide, the whole area looking like some winter scene with snow covered mountains. The limpets on the chalk were well attached here and would leave an indent even as much as a few centimetres wide, in the chalk where they had been attached.

Further along the beach there was an area where the cliffs contained bands of London clay. Often she would find the odd clam and lots of shells of slipper limpets playing piggy back on their fellow mates. You could get as many as six all attached to one another. She had to be careful in this area as in places the clay sand mixture was very soft and on one occasion she sank down nearly to her knees and had to leave her boots in the mud in order to escape. She now carried a small stick useful to prevent her slipping on seaweed covered rocks and more importantly for checking the softness of the beach she was walking on.

Many of her shells were obtained from nearby fisheries which daily trawled for clams and oysters. However, many oysters were now cultured in oyster farms or imported from Europe. The fisheries prepared these for transport around the country and overseas and the shells were often discarded in huge piles on the edge of the shore. These provided a marvellous resource for Annie and free to collect. She would often fill up two bags to the top full of shells and sit on the bus, much to the annoyance of some passengers who could not stand the fishy smell and lack of space. She just smiled and ignored them. She'd tried to spray some eau de cologne over them which she had brought with her, but that made little difference to the smell.

At home she had a gas ring in the shed with a big pot on top. She would throw her shells into boiling water in the pot to clean them, but not the very delicate tellins or cowries which were clean already. Some shells were black due to oil or other causes and these were rejected. Once boiled good shells came out white as porcelain, the entire weed etc. boiled off. They were then piled up to dry in her warm conservatory where she had a large mahogany refectory table covered in a cloth, where she assembled them into different items. She would use single shells in some cases, especially winkles, to paint eyes on them and give them cotton tails to represent little mice which children loved to buy. Teeny cowries were treated the same way to become teeny mice and slipper limpets sitting on top of each other were also given eyes and tails so that they looked like a group of menacing mice. The odd limpet and cockle shell was also treated in the same way with eyes but had four cotton legs and a tail to represent a tortoise. Whelks were used for bigger mice or played a part in the internal structure of other models.

A strong glue was used when assembling groups of shells. Often models could take several days to assemble and for the glue to dry and then they often had to be painted or faces were put on them. She made spectacular shell towers often using different sized bottles as a centre support. She would arrange shells in all sorts of patterns - zig zags, whorls, stripes, each being very effective. She also sometimes would edge the shells using a fine brush with gold paint to give them even more effect. Shells could be used to represent all kinds of things. Mussels could be arranged open side upwards in wreaths or used as petals for flowers with razor shells for stems. Large cockles or clams could be used to represent bonnets behind other shells being used for heads. Cockles could also be used to represent the two large eyes seen in owls. All her goods were sold in the window of her little shop which was on the road down to the harbour. She did very well in summer as people would always pass by the shop on their way to book boat trips to watch seals, birds, to fish or visit local islands. Most of her work was done on Sunday afternoons or in the evenings. In the winter, when the town was deserted with very few visitors, she would thread cowries together using strong cotton to make small placemats. She did not go onto the beach. In the winter she would spend her time building up her stocks ready for the Easter opening.

3 TIME AND TIDE WAITS FOR NO-ONE

Summer came and Annie was very active. She walked down the stone steps from the promenade at the top of the cliff past the purple and white flowers of the sea campion and the large leaves of the sea beet now covered in snails and cabbage white caterpillars. In the summer purple valerian bloomed forth and fields of rice grass bowed in the wind covered the cliff. The path ran down through the winkled and barnacle covered rocks. Annie passed the zone of fibre like cladophora sea weed sprinkled with toothed wrack and sea lettuce. Once on the beach she passed the paddling pool which was topped up by the sea every time it came in. The council, every spring, would clear out the rocks and stones from its base that had been washed in during the winter so that children could swim. Gulleys of chalk, formed by faults in the chalk surrounded the pool. Each gulley had pieces of flint embedded in them and small pools as they ran down to the sea. Man-made gulleys ran from the back of the paddling pool to help the overflow when the pool was full. After the milky appearance from the chalk had settled the pools were very attractive with their pink tufted coralline seaweed along their rims studded with bright green sea lettuce. Piles of dislodged flints were located at the front of the pool, some contained fossils such as sea urchins from the late cretaceous period. At the low tide mark Annie would see the bootlace weeds mixed with palm like oar weed. With the movement of the tide they writhed like snakes, their thick brown stalks waving to and thro.

Annie made her way along the strand line picking up shells, brushing off the sand and other debris and putting them into her red bag. She used to just put them in her bag, sand and all but this increased the weight and proved bad for her arthritic knees, and her garden was not doing that well with all the waste sand dumped on the soil each time she came back. She used her rake to dig out some of the deeper shells and also to lift up the piles of weed, whelk cases, dead crabs and other flotsam and jetsam along the strand line. Sometimes she would find the odd mermaid purse the egg cases of rays or skates or dogfish sometimes even with young inside not destined to make it any further. The gulls already had done their morning sift of the weed for food but many now relied more on people feeding them back in the town. It was not yet the time for them to have young with them so the defensive HA HA HA could not be heard. Annie had survived swooping gulls all her life and I think many of them were used to her by now. Sometimes she would bring stale bread with her to feed them if she had any left.

She picked up her trailing skirt which was already wet from the wet sand. She had tied her shoes around the neck to put on again when she climbed over the rocks.

A flock of sanderlings flew past her giving their small staccato sounds and the odd pied wagtail made attempts to catch flies in the weed. Anne liked the sound of the mournful cry of the curlews in the estuary and with the lapping sound of the waves felt this was perfect bliss and wished she could be lulled to sleep by these sounds. On her travels over the beach she would sometimes pick up a pretty stone, especially if it had patterns on it created by crystals of pure white or orange coloured quartz. Sometime pieces of coal or slate were washed up and on rare occasions sea beans which had travelled for thousands of miles from as far away as Mozambique.

On she went scratching away at the strand line until she came to the edge of the rocks surrounding the raised hill known as the fort. This had once been the home of a lord but was now an empty shell, the oak door and other features removed many years before. The metal hand rail running from the top onto the beach was now rusty and only individual parts remained. It's said that once rust starts it sends an electrical current through the whole metal work which will also encourage rusting. This is seen in the metal fencing, often parts of it now only thin strands like wire.

She reached the base of the rocks which were part of the island just adjacent to the beach. Many little shallow pools surrounded the rocks and she picked up shells lying in the bottom of these. Through the island ran a rocky cave which the sea passed through when the tide was in. One could see by the height of the barnacles and limpets and the lines of red sea anemones on the rock surface that at high tide the sea reached nearly to the roof of this cave. As a child Annie used to touch these large deep red anemones with tentacles retracted which responded by squirting out water at her. Small green worms also ran between the weeds and sand flies flashed their reflecting wings to mates while playing in the weeds. Often near the little pools in the rocks one could find sea bristle tails. Also in very small pools in the barnacle studded rocks one could find small grey petrobius, (sea springtails) floating and attracted to each other because of their waxy coatings. They would and spin round and round helplessly in the centres of these pools.

Annie liked walking through the cave as it was shaded in hot weather and often there were piles of shells washed inside for collecting. There were large rocks on the base of the cave left over from rock falls and a large central pool where one had to crawl past to reach the other side. Often other sea creatures would be trapped inside this pool as the tide retreated. On one occasion hundreds of starfish covered the cave floor and the rocks giving the cave a bright orange appearance. The far side of the cave often would have the tide partially in. so that looking through one could see a beautiful blue sea with the odd passenger boat passing by. Gulls and other birds fluttered about on the grass covered cliffs above, often making their nests there. Seals would sometimes sit on the flat lower rocks of the island which protruded out to sea and were never totally uncovered.

Often with an oncoming tide the first third of the beach would be covered in two hours, whilst the second in one hour and the third very quickly. Today she entered the cave. The roof and sides were still dripping with sea water mixed with water that had drained through the surface of the hill. She edged her way past the pool to the other side of the cave. Little did she notice that the tide was coming past the entrance to the cave. There was an abundance of shells this day. Previous storms had washed many of the creatures from off the rocks and this had provided food for other sea creatures which ate them. Her red bag by now was very full so she turned to go back so as to return home. By now the sea was deep on the outside but she had been in this situation before. She waded out into the sea and tried to lift her bag and skirt above the waves but failed. She made her way to the shore swinging the bag side to side to give her momentum against the oncoming waves. She had to make sure that she reached the beach safely as on the corner there was a deep pool where children would play when the tide was out. This became a whirl pool which was well known as a danger by small boat owners.

She staggered up the beach her clothes and bag now heavy with salty sea water. Luckily it was not far from her home just up the little hill leading from the harbour. She would have to wash her clothes that day so she would be ready to take her shell models to the local market the following day.

4 THE WOODEN BOOK

Sunday had come and Annie had been to church for an early service.

The sea had been rough the previous night, the wind rattling windows and shop signs squeaking as they swung to and fro. The rain beat down on the roofs and gutters and the drains were overflowing. One could hear the waves pounding against the rocks. But now all was calm but lots of things had been washed up on the beach. Whole trunks and branches of trees were washed in as well as pieces of wood with ship worm or barnacles attached. The sand was still so wet that Annie's feet sank down as she stepped onto the beach. There were lots of large pools scattered around and many shells. She did her usual trip along the beach past the padding pool and walking up towards the cave. Just at the side of the cave the tide was retreating. Looking out to sea she could see something bobbing up and down in the waves. It came in closer and she paddled in the water and managed to grab hold of it. It looked exactly like a book but made of wood. It had a Paris sticker on the front and must be hollow inside as something rattled when she shook it.

With great difficulty she put it in her bag so as to take it home to examine it closer. She carried on collecting shells for another fifteen minutes and then left. She then climbed up the hill to her shop. She lived alone down stairs in a room at the back of the shop which had the kitchen and conservatory in the back. She lit her gas lamp as it was getting late and put her bags onto the table in the conservatory. She warmed up some soup and cut some brown bread with two slices of cheese to go with it.

After her tea she pulled out the wooden book from her bag and put it on her table. It was very light there were no pages as the sides were wood. She turned it upside down and something inside dropped to the bottom. The whole hollow box was sealed. She tried to open it but there was no hinge or sliding compartment or small door. What was it for she wondered and laid it back down on the table. It wasn't a jewel box, it wasn't a small coffin, it was never meant to be read, but it still looked like a book

The wooden book had been hidden dusty on a shelf for over three hundred years in an old museum library in Paris It had no title on it spine so was never chosen to read especially as it was on the top shelf over five metres from the floor and could only be reached by a moving ladder. Its light brown colour also made it insignificant but little did people know it was significant. The front had a brief title covered by a large label. It had been through the Napoleonic wars and was nearly was destroyed during the French revolution when many books were piled up and burnt. It was smuggled out with other books with treasured artefacts from the museum on a ship bound for England. The ship was shipwrecked on rocks near the Cornish coast but the books were held in a lead box which survived under the sea for years until finally the leaden box broke open and the wooden book was the only item that floated to the surface to be washed onto the shore to be picked up finally by Annie shell hunting.

Why was this item made to look like a book? What was inside or was it just a novelty? There were no ways of entry and if there were it would not have floated to the surface of the sea. Annie was determined to get to the bottom of this.

5 HIDDEN PROPERTIES

Annie had tried to open the box with her mother of
pearl handled pen knife she used for opening shells
There was no easy access, every edge was sealed tight.
Annie took her knife and heated it over the oil lamp.
She ran it down the edge of an inside rim to burn
through the glue. She then took the knife and eased
up one side. Suddenly one side flew up and over.
Annie stepped back before she looked inside. Inside
was a small seal covered in red wax paper. She picked
it up, the ribbon that had once held it attached to the
box was now in tatters, showing that is was very old.
She picked off the thin paper covering the seal. On
the seal were many circular patterns and the words in
Latin, Vox Populi,Vox Dei which she knew from her
Latin at school meant the voice of the people is the
voice of God. What a peculiar thing she thought and
as she said this there was a whirring noise and a long
soft sound rather like a sigh. She threw the seal back
in the box and shut down the lid. She decided to
make a pot of tea and some food. The seal she felt
was useless, she had seen better patterns on her shells
and on seals in a museum.

 She had a few days ago collected lots of whelk shells
so she decided the book box would be ideal and
much more useful for holding these. The whelks were
all over the table and really in the way. With a

sandwich in one hand she used the other hand to start throwing the whelks into the book box. It filled them so full that there was hardly room left for the seal as well. She shut down the lid and put a large rubber band round it to keep it shut.

She put the box on a shelf and settled down in an arm chair to finish her sandwiches and pot of tea. She must have dozed off and thought she had dreamt of being close to the sea shore. She could hear the waves lapping up onto the shore and the mournful cry of a seagull. She was awake and could still hear the sound. She looked all around the room until she found where the sound was coming from. It was the box. She undid the rubber band, flung open the book box's lid and was blasted by the sound of the sea and gulls. It was not just a single rendition but many renditions all together with similar sounds. She picked up one of the shells and found it was coming from inside it although it was diminishing and then stopped suddenly. The other shells gave the same sound. She had always been able to hear the sound of the sea when she put the shells close to her ear but this was different, she could even hear the waves splashing on the shore and had never heard gulls before. She replaced the shells in the box and they started making a noise again. She decided to take all her shells out and put them onto the table. They all sang their tune for a while but then it stopped. When she put the seal next to them they started up again.

Putting them back into the box the sound faded away eventually but if she put the seal back in the box they would start up again. It seemed, in some way, the seal itself could help produce sound from the shells. She took the seal out as she was determined not to have the shells singing again. She moved the oil lamp which had been in the family for many years next to the seal so as to have a good look at the writing again. As soon as the seal touched the base of the lamp she heard another noise which sounded like talking. She listened carefully and to her astonishment recognised the voice of her own mother who had passed away several years ago. This gave her quite a start. She then tried other objects in the house and conversation could be heard for these too when she touched the seal against the object. Each seemed to have different properties depending on the use of the item. Those items which were well used gave a clear recording while those which had not been handled much only retained a part of the conversation from their last owners. Many of the conversations were just general comments but some from some personal handed down items were interesting and may have been other relatives, possibly even her father who had been killed in the war when she was a child and she had never heard him speak.

Her carpet in the house was deep red, worn more where she sat and overall a bit faded. On the table was a chenille red table cloth with the oil lamp on.

The wooden fire surround had sides like Greek pillars. Two brass candle sticks were placed on either side with a photo of her late husband in the centre. A small round table next to her arm chair was covered by a lace white cloth stained brown with numerous spillages of tea.

On shelves around the room she had many ornaments which she had bought or was given over the years. Some of these had been inherited from her in-laws and probably handed down through the generations.

There were several statues of saints, one being St Francis with animals at his feet and in his hands. Another was of Jesus with a red sacred heart in the centre of his chest. There were large tropical conch shells, the content of which would have been cooked and eaten. There was a plaster black dog which she had won by throwing bean bags at tins in a fair. The black dog always reminded her about Winston Churchill's bouts of depression 'His black dog days'

No item was exempt from having an inherent sound when she touched it with the seal. She also decided to put a new ribbon on the seal so she could wear it around her neck like a trophy. She valued it above all the things she had ever found and it gave her a new impetus and a desire to try it out on anything she came across. She could feel the vibration inside the seal when it touched an object. It started out slowly and then reached a peak but faded after a few minutes as the speech was lost. Some 'recordings' were much stronger than others and the words nearly word perfect. Some had recorded laughter, sadness or joy. She imagined the person had held the object at a certain time while speaking or making a remark to themselves or someone else and in some way the object had recorded the speech.

She had read in a magazine once at the hairdressers an article about the 'Stone Tape Theory. Here some recordings of a manifestation were captured and would, under certain circumstances, cause past events to be replayed for people to see. It was assumed that they were closely connected to that locality in some way and what was seen was an echo of an event. The sound produced by touching the object with the seal could probably be the same sort of phenomenon. She remembered the words of Christ who said on Palm Sunday on entering Jerusalem that even if the Pharisees stopped the people singing the rocks and stones would start to sing hosanna. The seal's activity in some way acted as a transducer releasing energy as sound from the object. In the 1960s an archaeologist, TC Lethbridge, proposed that even water was able to record strong human emotions and release these to people in some circumstances. Most objects contain some water as do we, having 90%. Research suggested that some sort of electromagnetic charge is present which holds memory and releases this to certain susceptible people. Annie was very familiar with the sound of water in all sorts of circumstances being down on the beach nearly every day in storm or fine weather. It was suggested that the person could, in handling the object, exhale water droplets onto the object so that they become part of the fabric. A person picking up the object could then inhale the water droplets so they become part of its fabric. The water molecules and the message transported from their lungs to their brain. But Annie was not picking thoughts up in her brain; she could actually hear people talking. Some sort of disturbance usually can release ghosts but Annie was just picking up conversation. Possibly her body also triggered initiation of a process for the seal to release this phenomenon. It had been demonstrated that when water is exposed to electromagnetic fields it can amplify signals many times. The electric field produced by the human heart and probably other organs in the body can be detected by a glass of water placed a few feet away. The whole density of water can be changed, it is believed, by sending ones thoughts to it.

Annie, through her curiosity, had tested all the objects in her house. Many of the objects did not have recordings either because they had not been near a conversation or had not been handled much. Metal objects gave no response possibly because any energy present may have been discharged through the handler and sent down to earth rather like a lightning.

By placing the seal against an object it would act as a conduit for sound like a loudspeaker. Being portable and held with a ribbon this now meant that Annie could take it to other places to try it out.

She went to a charity shop and in a corner next to the bric a brac quietly lifted out the seal from under her blouse and put it onto a large blue vase. The hollow inside of the vase helped to magnify the voice produced and it echoed round the shop giving the charity volunteers such a shock that they ran into the back room. Annie left quickly before they had time to question her. She went to several other charity shops to buy oddments and take them home to see what information they would produce. Some of the conversations were very sad as the objects had been donated by people who had lost parents. Others were general comments but also some seemed important to the person. She even found that some of her shell ornaments could produce her own voice if she touched them with the seal. It was lovely to know that the shell ladies she made would now hold her voice. She felt that they really were a part of her and was so glad that she had spent many patient hours constructing them.

6 VOICES FURTHER AFIELD

Objects made of plaster were especially good at
retaining conversations possibly as they held the most
water she thought. She had won two large Alsatian
dog plaster castes at a local fair once and these echoed
the noise and excitement of the fair and in doing so
brought back memories of the good times with her
family. These good results from plaster casts also
seemed to be confirmed when she took a day trip by
coach to the Victoria and Albert museum in London.
Many of the busts of famous people and others
produced a jumble of conversations derived from the
many visitors who had touched them in passing.
Michelangelo's David cast in plaster had been
touched on the feet by many passers-by as had the
reproduction of Trojan's column with its first century
reliefs. She found it interesting when she reached the
two statues in Portland stone of Melancholy and
Raving Madness. These had been on the gates of the
17th century mental hospital. She could hear loud
noises and even some screams in the background of
the recordings. Not all the conversations were in
English, especially from those casts made overseas.
An example was the Roman portrait busts. What she
did find interesting in the Indian section of the
Victorian and Albert museum was Tipus tiger, a

wooden model of a tiger eating a European in the 1790s. It had previously been kept in the East India Company's museum. Turning the handle inflated the bellows pumping air into pipes to make a growling sound of a tiger and the cries of the victim. The left arm also rose to cover the mouth and lowered again. Inside was also a miniature organ but was not working. Annie could hear conversations from the English occupation as well as more recent sounds of laughter and astonishment at the noise it made.

In the centre of Annie's home town there was a large square with a Victorian water fountain under which was a horse trough which had been donated by the local council. There were fewer horses these days except for the ones used to transport visitors around the town. But donkeys on their way to the beach would make use of the water in the trough especially on hot days. Also in the square was a large yew tree now divided into two. Next to the square was the church and this yew tree originally was in its ground but now this had been paved over to become part of the square. Its origin, Annie was told, came from the site where the church was now. The tree dated back to the time of the druids when they planted yews by temples or where cells of early saints were found. The tree was unstable on one side and had been propped up by large buttress like shoots growing from the base of the trunk. This tree had railings around most of it but for an open section which led to a hollowed out section inside the tree where there were placed two benches. Often these benches were covered in red berries from the tree, the fruit was not poisonous but the seeds and leaves of the tree were and are best avoided. Annie remembered how she had visited Down House in Kent where there was a huge tree close to the house and wondered about its safety for the Darwin family. The tree in the square provided a thick canopy and blackbirds loved to eat the berries on the yew tree and would sit in the trees for hours singing a whole medley of different songs. The yew was used by archers for long bows in medieval times and for Christians represented the resurrection as it could regenerate from any part and heal itself if damaged. All other trees and bushes previously surrounding the yew had long gone, dying out through changes in climate and age.

Annie sat down in the middle of the tree on her way home one day. She still had the seal around her neck held by the new ribbon. She had been walking around the church seeing if she could pick up voices produced by some of the monuments in there but with little success. Her shell collecting and modelling had been put on hold for a while. Under the yew tree she heard a voice and was surprised as there were no other objects around. She remembered what she had read that some believed that apparitions etc. could be stored in the water held in trees. She listened carefully and heard the words repeated again and again. It sounded like someone in a desperate tone of voice saying 'message in tree'. She walked around the tree but could not find anything carved into the tree. What did this mean? She could not work it out. She went to see her old friend George. He used to be a tailor in the town His house was quite unusual. Every room contained several sewing machines. He collected them as he was fascinated by the precision workmanship. He was proud of his collection and also had a collection in his conservatory. He had covered the glass windows in there with fluorescent plastic pieces so as to give a selection of colours when the sun came through rather like stained glass windows. He had a table there where he sat to maintain and mend his sewing machines. He called Annie in and they sat down for a cup of tea. Annie related her tale but not wanting to be thought mad she did not mention how she could listen to past conversations. She asked if he knew what could be meant by a message in a tree. He said he could not think of anything but remembered that when young he had been to the site of the Garden of Gethsemane where there was an olive tree with a hole in the trunk where people posted their prayers. George asked Annie if she had looked for any holes in the tree and she said she hadn't. George said he would come with her to see if there were any cavities in the yew's tree trunk. He put on his heavy grey overcoat, hat and his scarf and they both made for the town square. As the yew was centuries old there were many nooks and crannies in the trunk.

George put his hand inside several of these but many were full of wet decaying wood. The remnants of a birds nest was in one of them. He then tried a narrow crack quite high up in the tree hardly noticeable from the ground and pulled out what looked like a bit of slate which he was just about to throw away when he noticed some writing on its surface. He showed Annie but neither could decipher the writing and decided to take it back to George's house. Once inside they placed the slate in a bowl of water and gently rubbed away the dirt on its surface. Much of the writing had been lost they could not make it out but the words chamber, underground and Harbour Heights stood out. George immediately said he remembered his mother telling him about Harbour Heights. In its time it was a grand hotel with many luxurious rooms. The entrance was said to have been so extravagant with majestic concrete lions either side of the door and huge Victorian globe-like lights inside the hallway. His mother said that many important people had stayed there and it was very expensive for its time. Each room, she would say, had four poster beds and drapes that were red and had gold embroidery and tassels in them. The restaurant served exotic international cuisine and used fine silver service. George had in his possession one of the silver gravy boats that they used in the past which was inscribed with a crest and the name of the hotel. He had not polished it for a while and it was black with time. Someone in the town also had some of the

marble statues that used to decorate the elaborate
fireplaces in the hotel. It was a grand house near the
harbour but people said that because of its bright light
which escaped during the black out, it was an easy
target for German bombers in the war. Because of
this it received a direct hit by a bomb during the war
but fortunately it was winter with few guests present
at the time. A new, smaller guest house had been built
several years ago on the front part of the land but the
back was just wasteland, a place for numerous tall
buddleia plants, brambles, black birds and foxes.
Annie recalled that she used to play in this area as a
child and did he know anything about any
underground passages, cellar or anything. He said he
did not know and the whole area was now fenced in
to prevent trespassers being injured in the debris still
left there.

Annie, after lots of persuasion, got George to try and
take her inside this fenced off area. They did it at dusk
so nobody would see and brought torches for when it
got dark. Carefully they raised up the wire netting and
went through. Annie had brought a stick with her
which she prodded the ground through the
undergrowth. George had even brought some
secateurs with him to cut down the brambles. About
half way she noticed that a more hollow sound came
from her prodding and she knelt down with George
to clear away the rubble, George was complaining he
had been stung by nettles and scratched by brambles.

On the ground there was a flat surface covered in moss which they scraped away to reveal a wooden trap door. It must have been oak as it had not decayed so had survived but they could see it was rotten at the edges. They cleared away more rubble and George managed to get his hand under one end of the door and lift it up slightly They both took hold and pulled it up, cutting away the roots that had grown across it. This door was large. George said it was possibly part of an old cellar or old priest hole. They shone their torches down but could not distinguish much. George slid himself down to the floor. Inside it smelt very damp and he could see that the floor was solid. Annie held a torch to help him get his bearings. The walls were black and he felt his way around the chamber. The walls were very bumpy as he touched them. Stalactites of lime hung down from the ceiling. Annie shouted down to see if he was alright and he replied that he was. He shone his torch at the wall to see what all the bumps were. He scraped off the black which smelt like soot and saw that all the walls were covered in shells of different kinds arranged in many amazing patterns. He shouted to Annie to come down and he helped her inside. He showed her the walls and she shouted for joy. She had seen something similar many years ago when her parents had taken her to Margate in Kent. Two boys had found a similar chamber with all the walls covered in shells. It was named the shell grotto. Here in this room there were also shells on the walls Annie had never seen before and must have been taken from other regions. At the far end there was a small black mass. George reached down to lift up what looked like cloth and stood back suddenly as there was a skeleton underneath. It must have been there for many years, possibly hundreds, and the material it was covered in, presumably clothing of some sort, was extremely fragile. It was getting late so they decided to leave and replaced the trap door concealing it again. The next day they took a member of the local museum to see and he was astonished at their find. The council became involved and during that year they restored and renovated the site making it accessible to visitors. Annie was praised and was top news for a week. The grotto was named Annie's Grotto after her.

7 ANNIE'S LEGACY

Annie carried on with her shell collecting and model making. It was March and the weather had not yet decided whether it would be warm or cold. There were long periods of sunshine but the wind could be cold. Annie had given up using her seal and it had been put on the mantelpiece. George was due to come round one evening as Annie had said she had seen an advert for a sewing machine in her paper. It was eight o' clock, with a wild wind blowing down her street towards the harbour. Trees were thrashing around and hotel signs were swinging for all they were worth. It had started to rain and showers came in intermittent sheets.

George had a key as Annie was deaf and knew she would not hear him knocking. He stepped into the hall which ran along her room which was the shop and made his way towards the back room. He could see a light at the bottom of the door so presumed she was inside. He took off his coat and hung it over the banisters on the other side of the hall. He knocked on the door so she would not be frightened if he just barged in. There was no answer so he called her name; he knocked again still no answer so he called her name louder. Again no answer so he opened the door slowly. As he did so he found that something was stopping the door from opening. He reached with his hand behind the door and felt at the base of the door on the floor. He pulled out the obstruction and saw that they were shells. He opened the door further again but there was some more resistance which he thought again were shells. He eventually managed to squeeze through and to his surprise he saw that the whole of the floor was covered in Annie's shells which she usually had stacked neatly in boxes on the shelves.

Had she had an accident of some sort or even a fit of temper and thrown them all over the floor. He noticed however that some were arranged in patterns on the floor. Perhaps Annie had done this purposely. Annie was nowhere to be seen. In the fire grate he could see what looked like an empty box which was nearly completely burnt and a small pool of wax with what looked like a ribbon attached. On the red chenille cloth all that was left was a large model of a shell lady standing proudly in the centre. Her dress was made of large scallops. The shell for her face had been painted with blue eyes, smiling red lips and flowing ginger hair and a small shell placed behind this to represent a bonnet. Under the lady was a scrap of paper which said 'For George'. Annie was nowhere to be seen in the house. Had she moved on without telling anyone? But no one had seen her move and her belongings were still there. Had she found out something from the voices that had sent her away on another quest or had she learnt something that could have helped her transmute time or dimension so as to live in some other dimension or parallel universe? No one will ever know; she was never seen again. George on his way out had picked up the shell lady. As he closed the front door he thought he heard the shell lady speak but he made nothing of it and went home. Visitors visiting the Annie's shell grotto have remarked that they have heard voices there and that one of them is a lady. George sits at home with the shell lady on his table waiting for her return.

Other books by Mike Pearce

Pattern for Purpose- God's and Man's designs
Red Fred Cell and Friends
Human Termites eat London
Pigeons Splat London
Glass Anemones Tentacle-ize London
Tuppeny Hangover
How to be a Successful Business Weed
I am Termite
How to Deal with Life's Snakes and Ladders
The littlest Oyster
Bits and Bobs
The Shell Man
Cats at Christmas
Tails,Tales
Pens for Pops
Trust-Nothing but a Must
In a Dark Dark Corner was the Holy Ghost

ABOUT THE AUTHOR

Dr Mike Pearce is a scientist interested in behaviour. He also was a lecturer in human biology and health at a college in Canterbury, Kent.

Made in the USA
Middletown, DE
14 May 2025

75556626R00027